Dear Parent:
Your child's love of reading

Every child learns to read in a different way ~~and at~~ ~~his or her own~~ speed.
You can help your young reader improve and become more confident
by encouraging his or her own interests and abilities. You can also guide
your child's spiritual development by reading stories with biblical values
and Bible stories, like I Can Read! books published by Zonderkidz. From
books your child reads with you to the first books he or she reads alone,
there are I Can Read! books for every stage of reading:

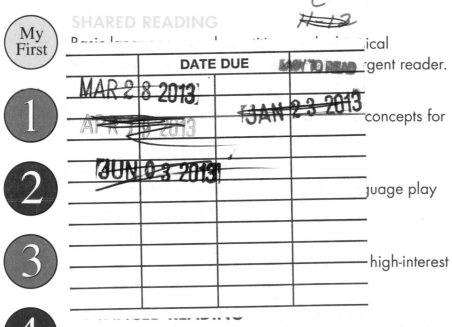

My First — SHARED READING
Basic lan~~guage~~ ~~...~~ ~~...~~ical ~~emergent~~ reader.

1 — ~~...~~ concepts for

2 — ~~...~~ ~~lang~~uage play

3 — ~~...~~ high-interest

4 — Short paragraphs, chapters, and exciting themes for the
perfect bridge to chapter books.

E
~~H-12~~

I Can Read! ~~books have been~~ ~~introducing children to the~~ joy of reading since
1957. Featur~~ing~~ ~~award-winning authors and illustr~~ators and a fabulous
cast of belove~~d characters, I Can Read! books set t~~he standard for
beginning rea~~ders.~~

A lifetime of discovery begins with the magical words **"I Can Read!"**

Visit www.icanread.com for information on enriching your child's reading experience.
Visit www.zonderkidz.com for more Zonderkidz I Can Read! titles.

Trust in the Lord with all your heart.
Do not depend on your own understanding.
—*Proverbs 3:5*

ZONDERKIDZ

Frank and Beans
Copyright © 2010 by Kathy-jo Wargin
Illustrations © 2010 by Anthony Lewis

Requests for information should be addressed to:
Zondervan, *Grand Rapids, Michigan* 49530

Library of Congress Cataloging-in-Publication Data

Wargin, Kathy-jo.
    Frank and Beans / story by Kathy-jo Wargin ; pictures by Anthony Lewis.
        p. cm. — (I can read! Level 2)
        Summary: Frank has always wanted a puppy, but when he is given an old
    hound, it takes the loneliness of the night to bring them together.
        ISBN 978-0-310-71847-5 (softcover)
        [1. Dogs—Fiction. 2. Night—Fiction. 3. Christian life—Fiction.] I. Lewis,
    Anthony, 1966- ill. II. Title.
    PZ7.W234Fn 2010
    [E]—dc22
    {B}   2009002871

Editor: Mary Hassinger
Art direction: Jody Langley

Printed in China

11 12 13 14 15 /SCC/ 10 9 8 7 6 5 4 3 2

Frank and Beans

story by Kathy-jo Wargin

pictures by Anthony Lewis

Frank rode his bike

past Mrs. Nelson's house.

There was a sign in her yard.

It said "puppies for sale."

Frank had always wanted

a puppy of his own.

His little sister Birdie

had a cat named S'More.

Frank rang the doorbell.

Mrs. Nelson answered.

She smiled and said,

"The puppies are in the backyard."

Frank saw the puppies right away.

They were black with white paws.

They had little ears and stubby tails.

Best of all, they were young and fast.

"Why can't I have a puppy, Mom?"

Frank begged.

"Puppies are a lot of work, Frank,"

his mom said.

"Maybe when you are older,"

she said with a grin.

Frank went to his dad.

"Maybe when you are older,"

Dad said.

Dad winked at Frank's mom.

The next morning,

Frank's parents woke him early.

"Surprise!" they said.

"Today you are older!

Let's buy one of those puppies."

Frank was happy and surprised.

But Mrs. Nelson looked sad

when they got to her house.

"I'm sorry," she said.

"I just sold the last puppy."

Frank was mad and sad.

He thought

he was getting a puppy,

and now he was not.

Mom put a hand on Frank's shoulder.

"It's hard to be let down,

but God wants us to have faith

that he will make things right."

17

Frank and his parents went home.

Soon, the doorbell rang.

Frank answered the door.

It was Mrs. Nelson.

She was smiling.

"This afternoon a friend asked me

to find a good home

for a special dog.

I thought of you."

She handed Frank a leash.

Frank's mother thanked Mrs. Nelson.

She said Frank would take care

of the dog.

"Frank, you are doing a nice thing
by caring for this dog.
I told you God makes things happen
the way he wants."

Frank frowned at the dog.

It was not a new black puppy

with perky ears and a stubby tail.

It was a grown dog

with long ears and short legs.

Frank was not happy.

He did not want the dog.

Frank's mom said,

"I'm sorry you feel that way, Frank.

But I am counting on you

to take care of this dog.

So is God."

That night, Frank's mom put the dog

on a blanket in the kitchen.

In the middle of the night,

Frank heard whining.

The dog was crying.

Frank listened.

The sound made him feel sad inside.

Frank went to the kitchen.

"What is wrong, dog?" asked Frank.

Frank petted the dog.

He could tell the dog was scared

to be in a strange place

with people he didn't know.

"Follow me, pal," said Frank.

In the morning,

Mom and Dad came to wake Frank.

Frank was still asleep.

The dog was next to him on the bed.

His parents laughed and said,

"You two go together

like franks and beans!"

"Well then," said Frank,

"I guess I'll call him Beans!"

And each time Beans saw a boy

with a new puppy, he felt glad too.